1 to 20, Animals Aplenty

For Mum

1 to 20, Animals Aplenty
Text and Illustrations © Katie Viggers 2014
First published in Great Britain by Eightbear Press

BROOKLYN
Published by POW!
a division of powerHouse Packaging & Supply, Inc.

Library of Congress Control Number: 2013951238

37 Main Street, Brooklyn, NY 11201-1021
info@bookPOW.com
www.bookPOW.com
www.powerHousebooks.com
www.powerHousepackaging.com

ISBN: 978-1-57687-680-0

Book design by Katie Viggers

10 9 8 7 6 5 4 3 2 1

Printed in Malaysia

1 to 20,
Animals
Aplenty

Katie Viggers

POW!

BROOKLYN

1 fox in a pair of socks

2

gorillas looking in mirrors

3 llamas *wearing* pajamas

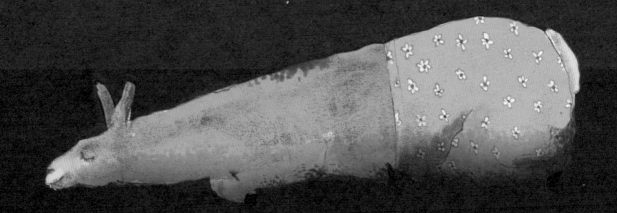

4
sharks
on
their
marks

gray reef

hammerhead

blue

great white

mountain

Boer

Nigerian dwarf

wearing coats

Angora

Nubian

6 baboons

hamadryas   yellow   Guinea

six
balloons

baby Guinea

olive

chacma

7 pigs

Berkshire

British Lop

Saddleback

7 wigs

Gloucester Old Spot

Ossabaw Island hog

middle white

Tamworth

8 bears

brown

sun

black
(North American)

panda

8 squares

polar

black
(Asian)

spectacled

sloth

9 cats in matching hats

american
shorthair

Exotic
shorthair

British
Bombay

Canadian
Sphynx

Siamese

Maine Coon

Ocelot

panther

lion

10 kangaroos

gray

red

in their favorite shoes

pug

King Charles spaniel

corgi

11 dogs

dalmatian

poodle

rough collie

Yorkshire terrier

dachshund

Chihuahua

and their pet frogs

greyhound

chow chow

12 racoons

with the baboons' balloons

14 capybaras

eating bananas

15
bats
who
are
acrobats

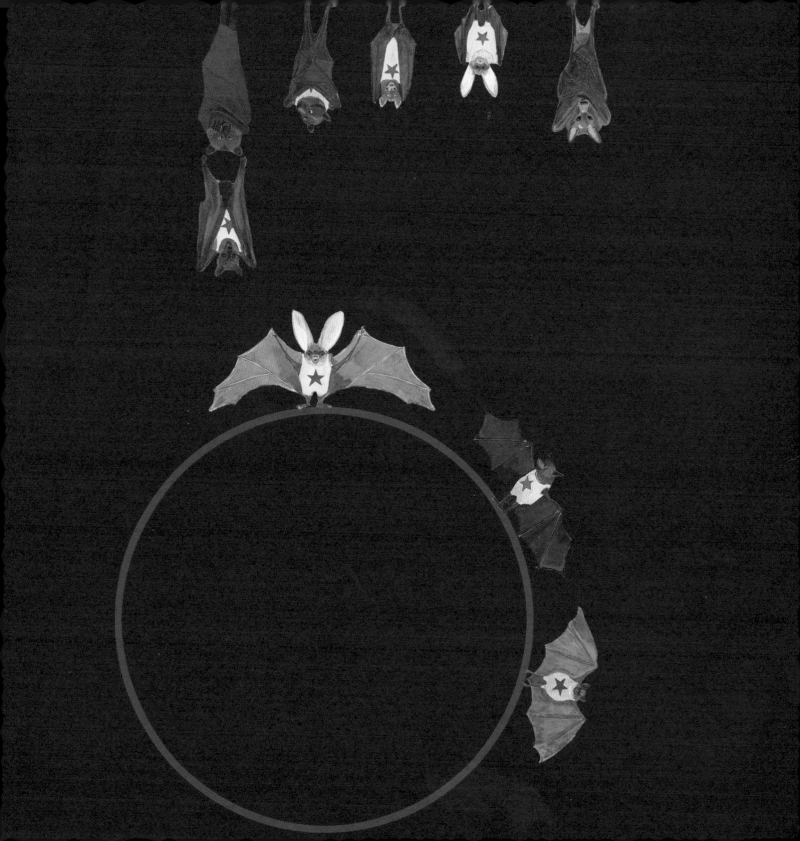

16
chickens

reading
Dickens

17 ants
in their
underpants

18 badgers

(American)

wearing badges

(European)

19 snakes eating cakes

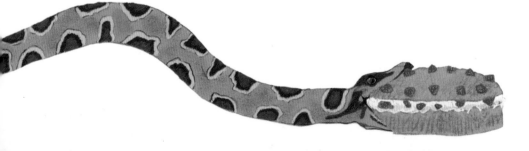

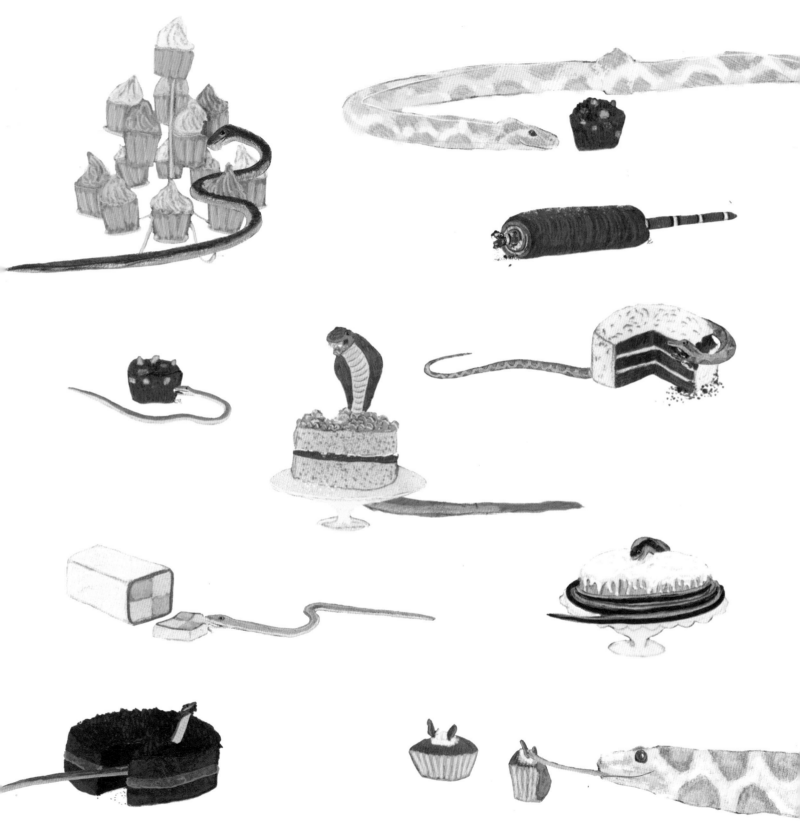

roadrunner bee eater ostrich seagull pigeon spoonbill toucan cockatoo blue jay canary

20 birds

kingfisher   cardinal   robin   pheasant   heron   crow   flamingo   hummingbird   kiwi   magpie

who have the last words

1

2

3

4

5

6

7

8

9

10

11

12

13

14

15

16

17

18

19

20

Katie

Viggers wrote this book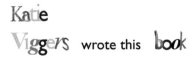

She grew up with lots of pets including 1  called Bob

2  called Simba and Henry

and 3  called Neville, Floss, and Spangles

She is an artist who lives in london, England